Praise for Newbery Medalist

Paul Fleischman
and
Bull Run

Winner of the 1994 Scott O'Dell Award
A Best Book for Young Adults (ALA)
A Notable Children's Book (ALA)
***Publishers Weekly*'s Best Books of 1993**
***The Horn Book* Fanfare List**

"A deft, poignant novel about the early days of the Civil War. . . . every detail here is used to great effect. From the great mass of historical material about the Civil War, and our many rather hazy ideas about it, Paul Fleischman has drawn a startling, instructive novel. His gallery of vivid characters reminds us that even the most overwhelming events are composed of the actions of individuals attempting to make sense of their times, and to shape them."
—*The New York Times*

"Powerful. . . . Reminiscent at times of the technique used to remarkable effect in the acclaimed PBS-TV series *The Civil War*, the novel relies on individual voices to give a human face to history. The result is at once intimate and sweeping, a heartbreaking and remarkably vivid portrait of a war that remains our nation's bloodiest conflict. . . . Fleischman's artistry is nothing short of astounding. This is a tour de force that should not be missed."
(Starred review)—*Publishers Weekly*

"Fleischman selects telling incidents to reveal character and to evoke the early course of the war and its impact on ordinary people. . . . An unusual, compelling look at the meaning of war." (Pointer review) —*The Kirkus Reviews*

"An impeccable piece of historical fiction that leaves the reader with a rich portrait of an important battle and the larger war which would follow. . . . Fleischman has done what he does best—create a unique piece of fiction with echoes of his poetry throughout." (Starred review)
—*The Horn Book*

"A remarkable series of vignettes. . . . Literarily, this work stands alone in juvenile and young adult fiction."
—*VOYA*

"Outstanding. . . . While the individuals are fictionalized, Fleischman's writing is so powerful that they spring to life. Unforgettable as historical fiction . . . an important book for every library." (Starred review)
—*School Library Journal*

"Excellent. . . . The book is graced with beautiful turns of phrase and a muted appreciation for the tragedy and absurdity of Bull Run, where soldiers maimed and killed one another while wealthy spectators sat enjoying picnics and champagne." —*The Washington Post*

BULL RUN

ALSO BY PAUL FLEISCHMAN

BULL RUN

PAUL FLEISCHMAN

Woodcuts by David Frampton

A Laura Geringer Book

HarperTrophy®
A Division of HarperCollins*Publishers*

Maps by Robert Romagnoli

Library of Congress Cataloging-in-Publication Data
Fleischman, Paul.
    Bull Run / Paul Fleischman ; woodcuts by David Frampton.
        p.   cm.
    "A Laura Geringer book."
    Summary: Northerners, Southerners, generals, couriers,
dreaming boys, and worried sisters describe the glory, the hor-
ror, the thrill, and the disillusionment of the first battle of the
Civil War.
    ISBN 0-06-021446-5. — ISBN 0-06-021447-3 (lib. bdg.)
    ISBN 0-06-440588-5 (pbk.)
    1. Bull Run, 1st battle of, Va., 1861—Juvenile Fiction.   [1.
Bull Run, 1st Battle of, Va., 1861—Fiction.   2. United States—
History—Civil War, 1861–1865—Campaigns—Fiction.]   I.
Frampton, David, ill.   II. Title.
PZ7.F599233Bu   1993   92-14745
[Fic]—dc20   CIP
                                                   AC

First Harper Trophy edition, 1995.

For Keith and all the Swards

BULL RUN

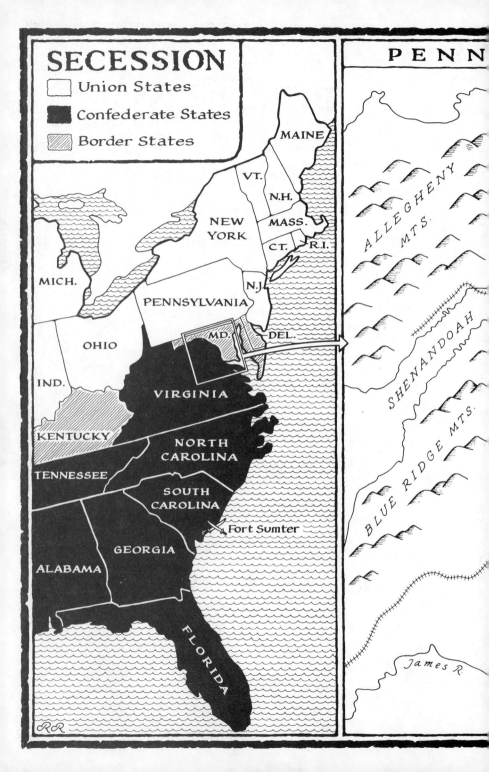

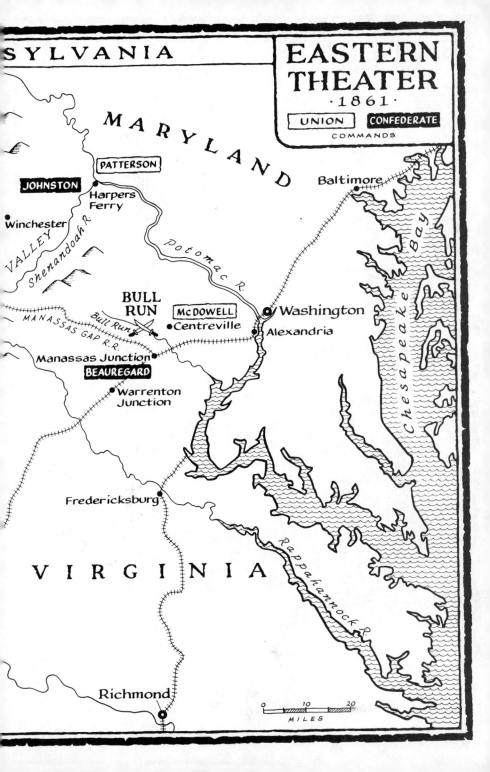

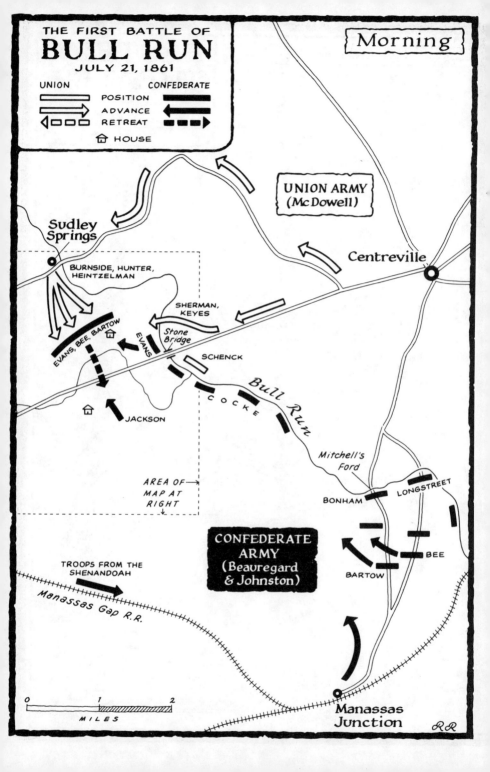

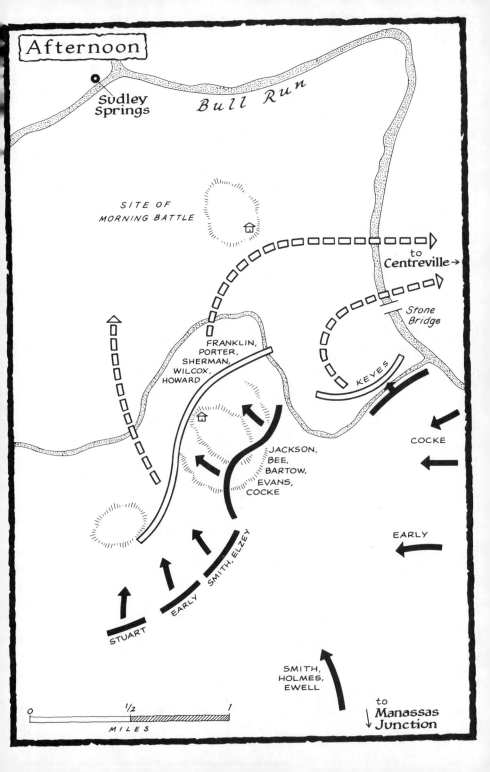

Afternoon

Sudley Springs

Bull Run

SITE OF
MORNING BATTLE

to
Centreville →

Stone
Bridge

KEYES

FRANKLIN,
PORTER,
SHERMAN,
WILCOX,
HOWARD

COCKE

JACKSON,
BEE,
BARTOW,
EVANS,
COCKE

EARLY

EARLY, SMITH, ELZEY

STUART

SMITH,
HOLMES,
EWELL

to
**Manassas
Junction**

0   ½   1
MILES

COLONEL OLIVER BRATTLE

The booming jerked me out of sleep, woke the dishes and set them chattering, and sent Clara dashing through the dark to the children. "Must be the Lord comin'!" cried one of the servants. I realized I'd been dreaming of Mexico. Strange.

I lit a candle. The clock read four thirty. All of Charleston seemed to be in the streets. I dressed, stepped out the front door, and was embraced at once by a teary-eyed stranger. "Praise the day!" he shrieked into my face. "They're firing on Fort Sumter!"

We gathered on Judge Frye's flat roof. The cannons rattled the very constellations. Shells sailed, their lit fuses tracing caliper-perfect arcs, then exploded. Each illumination of the bay was greeted with appreciative oohs and hurrahs. You'd have thought that the crowds were enjoying a Fourth of July display. Some brought baskets of food to the rooftops and raised glasses in toasts to South Carolina, Jefferson Davis, and General Beauregard. I was silent, though I shared their allegiance. I'd fought, however, fourteen years before from Veracruz to Mexico City. I remembered well what shells do to living flesh, and felt in melancholy mood. Amid all the cheering, the Negroes were similarly glum—suspiciously so. If they rejoiced that a war that might break their bonds had begun, they dared let no one discern it. By a bursting shell's light, I eyed Vernon, my body servant. He caught my glance and the slimmest of smiles fled his lips, like a snake disappearing down a hole.

LILY MALLOY

Minnesota is flat as a cracker. Rise up on your toes and you can see across the state. Scarce even a tree in sight but for a few willows beside the creeks. Father said God put willows here that man might have switches to enforce His commandments. Father was a grim-faced Scot and a great believer in switching. Each morning he put on his spectacles, without which he was all but blind. And each evening all six of us were whipped for whatever failings he'd noticed that day. If no fault could be found, we were whipped just the same for any wrongs committed out of his sight. Wee Sarah was not spared, nor Patrick, seventeen and tall. Father was taller still.

One chill April Sunday in 1861, we rode in to church and found a crowd before the door. Mr. Nilson was reading from a newspaper. Fort Sumter had been attacked. The gallant defenders had surrendered the next day. The President had called the Union to arms. That such a far-distant doing should, like a lever, shake Crow County amazed me. Mother wept. The men swore, despite the Sabbath. There was talk that a regiment of one thousand soldiers was being raised in Minnesota. Patrick's eyes glittered like diamonds.

Reverend Bott railed against the Rebels that day. His sermon's subject was "A man's worst foes are those of his own household." Father repeated the line at supper, his eyes fixed upon Patrick. That night, Father gave him a terrible thrashing. Afterward, Patrick asked the reason. "You're thinking to scamper off!" shouted Father. "Don't think I don't know it! And don't think you'll succeed!" He stood his full height. "I can see fifty miles! I'll hunt you like a wolf, and skin you like one!"

I didn't think I'd sleep that night. At dawn I woke to find my hand holding an old willow whistle Patrick had fashioned. I knew then he was gone and began to cry. We were five years apart but dear to each other. How I did fear that he'd be caught. Then I heard Father roar, "And the stone-hearted rogue took my spectacles with him!"

SHEM SUGGS

Horses have always served me for kin. The first time one looked back into my eyes, I knew that I was no longer alone on this earth, orphan or no. Never had one of my own to care for. The folks I lived with kept mules. But we'd put up wayfarers crossing Arkansas. Their horses trusted me straightaway, as if they'd known me from before. I'd feed 'em and wash 'em and brush 'em and we'd talk. An hour after arriving, they'd come to me sooner than to their owners. I felt among family with 'em, and forlorn as a ghost when they'd gone.

I was boarding at Mr. Bee's when a traveler told us about Fort Sumter. He left us a newspaper from Virginia. I was nineteen and couldn't read a lick, but I spotted a picture of a horse. I asked Mr. Bee to read the words below. They called men to join the cavalry. Mr. Bee hated Yankees the way a broom hates dirt, and he started in

again on Lincoln and the sovereign states and the con-
stitutional right to secede. I just nodded my head like a
wooden puppet, thinking about the newspaper instead.
It said they'd give me a horse.

GIDEON ADAMS

Though my skin is quite light, I'm a Negro, I'm proud of it, and I wept with joy along with my brethren at President Lincoln's call for men. How we yearned to strike a blow in the battle! Though the state of Ohio refused us the vote and discouraged us from settling, we rose to her aid just the same. No less than Cincinnati's whites, we organized meetings, heard ringing speeches, sang "Hail Columbia" and "John Brown's Body." All recognized that Cincinnati was vulnerable to capture. We therefore proposed to ready a company of Home Guards, its numbers, training, and equipment to be provided by the black citizens of the city and its services offered to her defense. At last the nation's eyes would behold the Negro's energy and courage!

We set up two recruiting stations. They were filled at once with scores of volunteers. Cheered by this magnificent response, we planned a second meeting at a schoolhouse. Arriving, I found the building all but ringed by a crowd of clamoring whites. Many had clubs. Several were drunk. "It's a white man's war!" one addressed me point-blank. "You'll do no damn parading about with guns!" I've tried to forget the coarser things said. I inserted the key in the door's padlock, but a police captain roughly drew it out. He announced that our meeting was canceled and our entire enterprise with it, on the grounds of inviting mob violence. "Go back to your miserable homes!" he ordered us, rather than the whites. "And stay there!"

I vowed that I would do otherwise.

FLORA WHEELWORTH

Lupine and honeysuckle bloomed as before, the oaks put out leaves, whippoorwills called. Outside it might have been any spring. But within the walls of the house it was the spring Virginia left the Union, a season separate from all before it. My three daughters came, with their families, and didn't their needles swoop like swallows, stitching up uniforms for their husbands. All the talk was of war, and all the singing. Each night we set candles in every window, proclaiming our joy at joining the Confederacy. "Nonilluminators" were suspect.

We remarked the train whistles coming from Manassas Junction while we sewed. The day arrived when we drove our men there to send them off to war. Each daughter held up her husband's sword and consecrated it with a kiss. Then they took their tearful farewells, and our brave knights boarded the train for Richmond, each followed by his servant. Banners flapped. A band played.

Women cut buttons off their clothes and handed them through the windows as keepsakes. The church society gave the men Bibles, each inscribed with "Fight the good fight." Girls whose beaus hadn't joined shamed them by giving out flowers to soldiers. Finally the whistle blew. The cars moved, drawing taut and then snapping dozens of parting conversations. "Stain your sword to the hilt!" shouted the waving woman beside me. Susannah, my eldest, scurried after the train. She'd supplied her husband with razor, mirror, hairbrush, nail file, calfskin slippers, and a fine suit of clothes to be saved for his triumphant entry into Washington. "Do *try* not to soil the coat!" she called out.

JAMES DACY

Never was there such a send-off as that given the Sixth Massachusetts Regiment, the first to leave for Washington. Thousands saw the trains off from Boston, the cheering loud enough to stir the saints. Great geysers were shot into the air by fire trucks when the cars passed through Worcester and Springfield. In New York, the regiment marched down thronged Broadway to an elegant breakfast at the Astor House. Their gunstocks were oiled, their bayonets bright. I was traveling with them as sketch artist for the *New York Illustrated News* and was similarly fitted out for the conflict, armed with paper and three dozen pencils. I was to send back drawings that would let readers stand where I stood and view the war as if there, lacking naught but the singing of bullets past their ears. I'd no notion I'd hear that sound so soon.

We reached Philadelphia that night and Baltimore the

following noon. We'd been warned that Baltimore was no Boston. Taking horsecars from one station to another, we were startled to see men and women wearing Confederate ribbons and rosettes. In place of cheers, we were greeted with insults. Plug-ugly toughs, spoiling for a fight, were drawn our way like moths to a light. The crowd about us thickened, grew bolder, then brazenly halted the horses. We disembarked and attempted to march. Vulgarities and vegetables were hurled. Rocks followed. Then deadly paving blocks. A Cambridge lad to my left was struck and sank upon one knee. A spectator tried to steal his musket. Then a shot rang out and a soldier just beside me fell to the ground. I'm a Boston man myself, and I snatched up the martyr's gun, hot for revenge. The company was ordered to fire on the mob. I joined them. There were screams, and further shots. We quick-stepped through a hailstorm of stones, finally reached the Camden Street station, then had to wait for a locomotive. Three valiant volunteers were dead. Many others were injured. I burned to put upon paper the faces of the taunting traitors and the fallen heroes, took up a pencil, tried to draw—but couldn't. My hands were shaking, with fury.

TOBY BOYCE

I was eleven years old and desperate to kill a Yankee before the supply ran out. It seemed that all Georgia had
joined except me. I knew I'd never pass for eighteen.
You can't very well lie about your height. Then I heard
that musicians were needed to play for the soldiers, any
age at all. I hotfooted it fifteen miles to the courthouse
and took my place in line. The recruiter scowled when I
reached the front. "You're a knee baby yet," he said. "Go
on home." I told him I meant to join the band. "And what
would your instrument be?" he asked. My thinking
hadn't traveled that far. "The fife," I spoke out. Which
was a monstrous lie. He smiled at me and I felt limp with
relief. Then he stood up and ambled out the door.
Across from the courthouse a band had begun playing.
We all heard the music stop of a sudden. A few minutes
later the recruiter returned. He held out a fife. "Give us
'Dixie,'" he said. I felt hot all over. Everyone waited. The

fife seemed to burn and writhe in my hand like the Devil's own tail. I heard Grandpap saying, as he had heaps of times, "A lie is a weed in the Lord's flower garden." Then that left my mind and I recollected him saying "Faith sows miracles." I found what seemed to be the mouth hole. "'Dixie,'" I announced. I closed my eyes. Then I commenced to blow and wag my fingers, singing out the song strong in my head. I believed it was coming from the fife as well, until I saw the faces around me. One man had his jacket over his head. The room echoed a considerable time after I'd finished playing. The recruiter's eyes opened slow as a frog's. I was surprised at his expression. "You've got spirit," he said at last. "And boldness. And pluck enough, I judge, to practice almighty hard, *starting today*." It was the first miracle I'd ever seen.

GIDEON ADAMS

The next day four of us marched to a recruiting tent to join the infantry. I happened to be the first in line. The enlisting officer had just asked me to sign when he noticed the hair curling out from my cap, saw for the first time that I was a Negro, and informed me in the most impolite terms that I could not be admitted as a soldier.

We left, despairing of ever fighting the South. Some of the men I knew put their pride in their pockets and joined as ditchdiggers. Some signed on as cooks or teamsters. Some stayed home, to hear once more that Negroes were cowardly, lazy, disloyal. I, however, refused to resign myself to serving with shovel or spoon. I would stand at the front of the fray, not the rear, and would hold a rifle in my hand. That recruiter had shown me the way.

I clipped my hair short that very night. The next day, I bought a bigger cap, one with a chin strap to hold it in place. Then I walked to a different recruiting station. The enlisting officer asked me my name. I foolishly feared he might recognize it. I looked up at a banner that read "One Thousand Able-Bodied Patriots Wanted," and gave him "Able" in place of "Adams." His brows furrowed at my fumbling reply. He asked me my age, then whether I'd any physical infirmities. He then asked what manner of service I intended. "Infantry soldier," I firmly replied. Perhaps I'd spoken too firmly. He studied me. I wondered if my cap had slipped. He said I'd be paid thirteen dollars a month and that the regiment would serve ninety days, time enough to whip the Rebels three times over, he assured me. He put his finger on a line in his roll book. I nearly signed my real name, and clumsily corrected myself. I stared at the letters. I was no longer who I was. The recruiter told me to return the next morning. I left in a daze, glancing at the white men around me, who thought me one of them. The dread of discovery streaked through my veins. I gave my chin strap a tightening tug.

VIRGIL PEAVEY

By Jukes, wasn't that a time! I walked forty miles with the rest of our company to catch the train to Montgomery. It was the first locomotive I'd ever seen. Didn't she come charging into the station, snorting steam like a dragon! "Mind the undertow!" someone called out. "Don't get sucked under!" I dashed away from the tracks for dear life. When I judged it safe, I scampered aboard, the whistle blew, and away we went. My, but we ripped along like the wind! Most all the passengers were soldiers. Those in the boxcars broke holes in the sides with their guns to see where they were going. Men hung out windows and climbed on the roof, yelling and singing and drinking all the while. We all knew that the war was as good as won. Northern ribbon clerks would never fight. America had cut free from England, and now we'd cut free from the Yankee tyrants and would be independent forever after. A white-haired schoolmaster riding in the car heard our talk and shook his head. Every secessionist's swaddling clothes are woven in Massachusetts, he said. His hobbyhorse is built of Maine cedar, his wedding ring worked by a Rhode Island goldsmith, his Colt revolver made in Connecticut, and his tombstone quarried in the hills of Vermont. There was silence. Then came a lively, democratic discussion, at the end of which we agreed not to throw him off the moving train, on account of his age, but to wait until we stopped at a station.

NATHANIEL EPP

I'm a dry-land sailor. Been from Maine to Mississippi. Horse, wagon, camera, and chemicals. I'd tie up, take portraits at twenty cents apiece, then move along down the road to fresh faces. In the spring of '61 the birds were bound north, but I was steering south for Washington. Soldiers by the thousand were camped there, and every one of 'em wanted his picture made.

It was May when I arrived. The city itself was nothing you'd want to photograph. The streets were shank deep in mud and slops. Cows were slaughtered beside the Washington Monument. The stench from the canals must have turned God's own stomach. But beautiful lilies rise out of swamps. It was in Washington that my luck bloomed.

I set up next to a Michigan regiment, and a boisterous, brawling lot they were. I painted a sheet with cannons blazing, hung it for a backdrop, set up my camera, and was swarmed with customers. How fiercely they glared! How proud their postures, each one a Caesar to himself and his family. That very first day I was taking the portrait of a Swede when some reveler fired off his gun and my subject fell dead on the ground. There was mourning and fighting. The man was carried off. I thought the portrait ruined by his moving, but developed it out of respect. It showed a blurry human shape seeming to step out of the standing man's skin. I nearly discarded it. Then a notion struck me. My heart commenced to flutter like a hummingbird. And that evening, like so many others after, I did a brisk business, at ten cents a head, in exhibiting what I billed to be the first photograph of the human soul, plainly leaving a dying body. I have never gone hungry since.

SHEM SUGGS

I walked from Arkansas clear to Virginia. I'd a time tracking down the cavalry, and when I did it was long full up. I told the officer I'd groom the horses. An hour above the knees and an hour below was the regulation. I was the only one who didn't complain. Other times, I mended saddles or doctored sick horses or watched the drills. It was grand to see the men ride in formations, sabers straight as church steeples. In the evenings they used them to roast rabbits and chickens. They were as fond of wagering as of food. They'd race horses any chance they got. If the ground was too muddy, they'd race sticks in the stream, and at night they'd pluck lice from off their blankets and race those, whooping 'em on like thorough-breds.

One morning a captain came up to me. There was measles in the camp and a man had just died. The captain led me to the man's horse, said that I could join

Company A, and walked away. The horse was named Greta. She was a small, bandy-legged gray. Teeth rotten. Ragged mane. Some might have waited for another man to die. But to me, no finer horse ever breathed. I stood where she could see me plain. My heart was pounding. "My name's Shem," I said. She lifted her ears. We gazed at each other. "I sure am pleased to know you," I said.

DIETRICH HERZ

For the first time in four years I didn't feel myself a foreigner. Nearly all the regiment was German. The welcome scents of sausage and sauerkraut rose from every cookfire at evening. We had good lager beer and the finest band in the camp. Visitors were surprised to hear our commands shouted out in German. None, though, could doubt our love for the Union. It had given us all a new life.

As when we'd first come to this country, the women had been left behind. From New York the boxes soon began coming. Jams, pickles, books, writing paper, thread, and a hundred other useful things were sent by the Soldier's Aid Society. I will always remember the first box that reached our tent. It was filled with linen shirts and handkerchiefs lovingly sewn by the women. We soon discovered that each held a note. One read "Brave friend, I pray for you daily." Others urged us to remain hopeful and healthy. All were encouraging, and cherished. Hearing them read, I felt I could see the women, merrily chatting while they sewed. The shirt I received was of fine workmanship, the stitches nearly invisible. When I opened it up, a photograph fell out. It showed the head of a woman, light-haired and young and most attractive. Then I noticed the note she'd enclosed, unsigned. I picked it up and felt suddenly cold. I did not read it aloud, like the others. It said only "I fear I will take my own life."

DR. WILLIAM RYE

Man is the deadliest of God's creatures. None could doubt it who'd watched the troops train. The recruits received guns and were shown how to shoot them. The use of the bayonet was explained. The cannoneer's craft was passed on from old to young—how to measure the fuses of shells that they might explode when amid the enemy, piercing scores of men with lead balls and scrap iron. How intently the men studied the art of killing. With what care their officers refined their skills through drilling, precision parades, mock charges. And yet, when the bugles are blown in earnest, how shocked we are that men bleed and die, as if we'd not striven day after day toward that very end.

My trade is healing, the opposite of a soldier's. Knowing there would indeed be bleeding and dying, I offered my services. My task was to keep a regiment of one thousand North Carolina men healthy. Many were felled long before we saw battle. The paths between their tents were sewers, the aroma conspicuous half a mile away. The men drank fouled water, were crawling with vermin, and tormented their stomachs with a gut-strangling diet of salt pork fried in rancid grease. Typhoid and measles raced through the ranks. Scurvy and pneumonia claimed victims as well. Dysentery was exceedingly common, and diarrhea all but universal. On many a day, fully one third of the men were laid low with illness. I felt defeat at each death, and consolation. Those who'd died, I told myself, at least hadn't lived to maim and murder countless other men in battle. It was a thought I never shared with the officers.

LILY MALLOY

Patrick entrusted Father's glasses to a peddler who was heading our way. The man returned them to Father the next week and predicted that Patrick would make a fine soldier. Father sent him away without purchasing so much as a pin.

The wheat grew up past my knees, then my waist. The sod house seemed dismal without Patrick, and I stayed outside as much as I might. I spoke to him when alone in the fields. I told him how much I missed him and how I wondered what he was doing and seeing. He heard my words. One day I walked to town, stepped into Mr. May's store, and was told a letter was waiting for us. My eyes went wide. It was from Patrick. I read it then and there by the window. He was camped, he said, outside Washington. He could glimpse a Rebel flag across the Potomac. He said he wished we'd seen him in his uniform, which had looked quite fine until two days before, when it had almost dissolved in the first hard rain. The vile profiteers who sold them would, he hoped, be hanged. The Minnesota men still lacked guns and marched with cornstalks on their shoulders instead. He described his day's schedule in detail and a game he'd learned, called baseball, in which one swung a stick at a yarn-covered walnut. His letter replenished me, as if it were food. I felt joined to him again. When I reached home and showed the others, they rushed to gather round, all but Father. He affected no interest at all and left. Yet when I reread the letter the next morning, I found his large thumbprints on all five pages.

TOBY BOYCE

I borrowed a fife, found a man to teach me, and commenced practicing from first light to night. For days I trudged up and down scales. Then through hymns. Then a songbook. After a week I told Grandpap good-bye, walked three days, practicing all the way, and joined the regiment's band. We played at a big review that first day. The tails of the coat they gave me scraped the dirt. I hadn't seen the music we'd be playing, but promised the bandleader I'd get through it. I did, not finishing much behind the others on most of the pieces and well out in the lead on "Dixie." The crowd cheered. I could scarcely believe I was part of the army at last.

I begged God not to let me miss the fighting. It was said we'd be marching North any day and would give our next concert in Washington. Five weeks later we were still in Georgia. We played at the dress parades every evening and when important sorts came to visit. We practiced some, but mostly the men spent their time gambling and brawling. Whiskey wasn't allowed in camp, but a woman used to come by, selling it from her special-made tin bustle. The cornet player poured liquor into a hollowed-out watermelon, buried it, and drank some each night through a length of straw. There was stealing and swearing and poker playing with cards that had Jefferson Davis and the rest of the Confederate big bugs on 'em. I feared for my life when the men got drunk. It was not the Christian life I'd known, and I began to wish I'd never left home. I recollected Grandpap saying that if I ever saw the Devil to cut him in half and walk on between the pieces. But if I'd done that, there'd have been hardly a man left alive in the band.

JAMES DACY

How I longed to render my drawings in color! To show
the red blouses of the Garibaldi Guards, the emerald
flags of the Irish Brigade, the tricolored standard of New
York's French regiment, not to mention the companies
of immigrant Germans and Scots and Poles, each with
their own vivid uniforms. And then there were the astounding Zouaves, who truly put my pencils to shame.
Baggy red pantaloons flapping like sails, leather leg-
gings, red-braided blue jackets, and atop every head a
red fez cap from which hung a long black tassel. They
were New York rowdies dressed in the style of the
Zouaves, the fearless soldiers of Morocco. Walking down
Pennsylvania Avenue, I stopped and gawked at the sight
of them, and watched one push his companion through
a barber's plate-glass window for sport. I'd heard tell of
their penchant for mayhem. But the following day I saw
Colonel Ellsworth lead them through the most difficult

of drills, perfectly synchronized, faultlessly executed, their rifles spinning at times like wheel spokes. It was a stunning display. I made several sketches and left sure that no army could best the Union. Walking toward another camp, I skirted some woods, heard a voice, then had my faith severely shaken. I'd come upon an officer, no doubt one of the many inexperienced civilians elected to his post. He was poring over a book, and was practicing shouting orders *to the trees*. The scene filled me with foreboding. I declined to present it to the readers of the *New York Illustrated News*.

JUDAH JENKINS

Colonel Elmer E. Ellsworth. The world knows his name. Songs and poems were written about him. Babies were named for him, and streets, and whole towns. His ugly face was even printed on envelopes. But what of James Jackson?

I grew up in Alexandria and was there the day the Union troops first dared to invade Virginia's soil. They skulked across the Potomac before dawn, riding on steamboats. We'd heard they might. I was eighteen years old and had stayed up all night waiting and watching from the attic window. They marched up from the river at dawn. When I spied the Zouaves, dressed up like peacocks, I thought I'd fallen asleep and was dreaming. Ellsworth sent a band of them to capture the telegraph office. Then he peered at the Confederate flag flying from the roof of the Marshall House Hotel. I saw him stride off in that direction and dashed down out of my house to follow. By the time I got there, he'd gone up the stairs, climbed out on the roof, cut loose the flag, and was heading back down the stairs with it. "I have the first prize," he shouted out. Mr. Jackson, the hotel's owner, met the intruder on the second-floor landing. "And I the second," he said, and killed Ellsworth with a shotgun blast. Straightaway, a Union soldier shot Mr. Jackson square in the face, then bayoneted him over and over in the chest, for the crime of defending his property. His blood was every bit as red as Ellsworth's, but who remembers his name?

Until that day I'd had doubts about secession. That evening I rode a horse to Centreville and joined the Confederates as a courier.

GENERAL IRVIN McDOWELL

I felt myself to be a horse who's ordered to gallop while still hitched to a post. As commander of the Army of the Potomac, I was expected to crush the Confederacy's army and, if need be, take Richmond, its capital. The public, the press, the politicians, the President—all demanded it. And since many of my soldiers were ninety-day men, whose enlistments would expire in July, I was expected to accomplish this with all speed. Despite the fact that my troops were as green as June apples, spoke a Babel of tongues, and were led by officers who knew nothing of battle. Despite lacking sufficient weapons, ammunition, mules, food, and equipment of every sort. Despite the fact that my success depended on keeping the Confederate army in the west from leaving Harpers Ferry and joining Beauregard, a duty given to General Patterson, who was too old and too timid for this or any task. Despite my not having a single reliable map of

Virginia, which I was to invade. And despite the most worrisome problem of all, one I dared not complain of in public: I, who'd just a few weeks before been made a brigadier general in command of an army of thirty thousand, had seldom led more than a hundred men.

In spite of all this, I drew up a plan of attack. It was approved by the President. We'd begin our march south in the second week of July. I dreaded the coming of that day.

FLORA WHEELWORTH

My daughters departed soon after their husbands. The house held but me and the servants once more. After all the bustling, I found idleness irksome and organized a Soldiers' Friend League. We sewed shirts by the score. We cut and rolled bandages. We searched our ragbags for scraps of linen and scraped them with knives to procure lint for wounds. While working we exchanged the latest news. General Beauregard, the hero of Fort Sumter, had come to Virginia and made his headquarters a few miles off in Manassas Junction. We felt as if the Lord had sent one of His angels to protect us from the Yankees. Mrs. Granger had actually spoken to him and reported him most charming. He was from French Louisiana and at once showed himself a gentleman by kindly advising all the civilians in Washington to leave, as he would shortly occupy the city. We prayed that he would do so quickly, for the newspapers said that the

Union was sending thousands of armed Negroes and Indians to pillage the South and free the slaves. Weeks passed. Our troops made no advance. We fretted and furiously debated but could not understand the delay. Then Miss Pruitt read from a Richmond paper a report stating that Lincoln so feared an attack that he slept with a guard of fifty men and had lately been drunk for days at a spell. Upon hearing this, we concluded that General Beauregard had been halted by his honor, which would not permit him to strike an opponent who was already all but prostrate.

GIDEON ADAMS

To be a Negro living in the midst of whites, unknown to them, is to be a ghost spying on the living. Oftentimes I felt I must have joined the Southern army by mistake. The soldiers mercilessly abused a stuttering black cook in our company and tormented the collie dog he'd brought with him. Most of them said they were fighting against secession, not against slavery. Some declared they'd rather shoot Negroes than the Rebels. My ears burned at such words.

In May we traveled to Washington. A march on Richmond was constantly talked of, but instead we merely crossed the Potomac and drilled on the south bank instead of the north. Unlike many of the men, I could write, and was often asked to take down their letters. I recorded their complainings about the heat, the drilling, the food, the lice. Many vowed to rush back to Ohio the moment our ninety-day term had expired, no matter if

the Rebels were marching on Washington. I nearly stran-
gled my pen at such times. Then one day I found myself
putting in ink a loutish private's opinion that the blood of
black people was thinner and inferior to that of whites,
which explained the Negroes' lack of intelligence. How I
hungered to yank off my cap and show him which of us
knew the alphabet and which was the inferior, ignorant
fool! I almost did so, and halted my pen. Then I mas-
tered myself and finished the letter, but closed it with
"Your wood-headed jackass" instead of the farewell he
dictated. He grinned, uncomprehending, at the words,
then below them scrawled, with some effort, his "X."

COLONEL OLIVER BRATTLE

In June I joined General Beauregard's staff to advise him on strategy. I found that he felt in no need of advice. Though his celebrated assault on Fort Sumter had been nothing more than target practice, he'd been hailed a hero so loudly that he'd come to think he deserved the name. He was a man who bore watching. President Davis knew this, and knowing as well that our troops were both unready and greatly outnumbered, forbade us to take the offensive. We were to pick a strong defensive position and block any Union advance on Richmond. We decided to make our stand along the southern bank of the stream called Bull Run. I studied its meandering course for miles. The banks were steep, the fords easily defended. The hills overlooking the terrain from the south would offer us a commanding position. But defense held little allure for Beauregard. In utter violation of his orders, he planned to cross the creek, outflank the

Yankees, cut them off from Washington, then take the city himself. He was short, like Napoleon, and believed himself to be as brilliant a general. In private, I feared that the similarity between them ended with their height.

A. B. TILBURY

By gravy, it was a glorious feeling! At last we were marching off to battle! All Washington crowded the streets something handsome. The regimental bands all blared. Standards fluttered. The summer sun glinted on bayonets by the thousands. We could no more keep from singing than from breathing. We filled the air with "Yankee Doodle" and "Rally 'Round the Flag, Boys" and "The Girl I Left Behind Me." Between them the shout "On to Richmond!" boomed up and down the ranks like thunder. Richmond was only a hundred miles off. We expected to be there in a matter of days. The thought stirred me. I'd come from Maine, joined up as cannoneer, and hadn't before been south of the Kennebec. I'd never known a Southerner either. But I'd read enough to know that they were cruel-hearted, warloving villains and that peaceable citizens like myself would have to take up the gun against them.

We crossed the Potomac and followed the troops who were on the south bank toward Centreville, twenty-five miles away. The day was as hot as the hinges of Hades. Our fine, straight lines wavered, then broke. Men wandered off to refill their canteens or chase chickens or rest in the shade of a tree. Blackberries were ripe along the road, and whole companies left ranks to pick them, singing and joshing all the while. I admit that I was one of them. Officers bellowed to no effect. Half of *them* ended up picking berries. It was less a march than a picnic ramble, with plenty of halts on account of the heat. As the men weren't accustomed to marching any distance, they soon felt the need to lighten their packs. The road became strewn with cast-off blankets and such. All day and on into the night we lurched ahead and lay down by turns. Finally we stopped and made camp. We'd completed our first day's march and were filled with pride in ourselves. Then a sneering captain informed us, with great disgust, that we'd progressed just six miles.

CARLOTTA KING

I come up from Mississippi with the master. He was a lieutenant, or some such thing. I heard him braggin' to another man that he had five thousand acres and loads of slaves, which was a bare-headed lie. And that his slaves would sooner die than run off and leave him, which was a bigger lie yet. Lots of the soldiers brought their slaves with 'em. We washed and cooked and mended, same as back home. Except we weren't back home. There were different flowers on the ground—northern flowers. The Union men weren't any more than a few hills away. I'd look at them hills. They did call to me powerful. I was a young woman and fast as a fox. I knew I'd surely never get another chance. I made up my mind and picked the night I'd go. My heart beat hard all that day. I didn't tell nobody. Then at supper another slave told how those that crossed over were handed back to their owners *by the Yankees*! My bowl slipped right out of my hands. I'd thought the Yankees had come to save us. I must have looked sick. They wondered over me, but I didn't tell 'em. I sat down by the crick.

I told myself I'd keep where I was—till the big battle, anyway. And I told myself to stop lookin' at the hills.

NATHANIEL EPP

With camera and wagon, I followed the army. It was three days before we reached Centreville. The village was small but the men's spirits high. They ripped down every Rebel flag, broke into houses, took what they liked. I saw a pair of them traipse back out to the road dressed up in plumed hats and satin gowns. Another, got up in a minister's garb, spoke Jefferson Davis' funeral service. Colonel Sherman rebuked them as Goths and Vandals and ordered them punished.

A few regiments went on to Bull Run, tested the Rebels, and were driven back. The men's mood changed when they got word of it. An ambulance wagon passed nearby, its passengers groaning for all to hear. The line for portraits grew suddenly long. The men looked glum. They knew they might die, and seemed desperate to see that they would live on, framed and set upon a table. That evening I announced that I would show my photograph of the human soul. The crowds were greater than ever before. An Irish chaplain paid his ten cents, viewed it, and praised my good works. I was pleased to see how the picture cheered the men. It had a similar effect upon me, for it brought in forty-nine dollars that night.

VIRGIL PEAVEY

We drilled in Alabama, then took the railroad to Harpers Ferry, Virginia. I was getting so used to trains that I fancied myself an engineer after the war. We joined General Bee's brigade, but all the talk was of General Jackson. "Old Lemon-Squeezer" the men called him. He was forever sucking on half a lemon. His peculiar ways went a long chalk past that. At night he was known to sleep under a cold, wet sheet to help his digestion. He was famous for his praying as well. Twice I saw him speaking a prayer while riding his horse, his eyes blank as a statue's. He was upright and religious to a dreadful degree. The first thing he did in Harpers Ferry was search out every barrel of liquor and pour it all to waste in the street. It was said that some men shed tears at the sight.

When we heard that Patterson's Union troops were coming, we streaked it to Winchester. They could make us move, but they couldn't catch us. It was a comfort to know they wouldn't find any liquor. Then our colonel announced that off to the east the Union army was moving in force and that Beauregard would be larruped without us. We marched twenty miles in eighteen hours, forded the Shenandoah River, then boarded a train on the Manassas Gap line. Old Patterson's probably looking for us still.

As soon as we stepped off at Manassas Junction the cars returned to bring more soldiers. We were told that we'd likely see battle the next day. Some men whooped. Some looked as solemn as General Jackson praying. My friend Tuck and I made a pact then and there to stay side by side when the shooting commenced.

GENERAL IRVIN McDOWELL

I spent a full day studying the terrain, revised my plan, and was ready to attack. Then I found that the army was out of food. The commissary wagons hadn't arrived. I squandered another day waiting for them, praying that Patterson had the Rebels in the west penned up beyond the Shenandoah. I made out the sound of train whistles far off, but thought little of it at the time.

All was finally in order. We would strike Beauregard on Sunday morning. On Saturday afternoon I was told that the Eighth New York Militia's term of service would end at midnight and that they planned to march north and not south. I addressed them, as did the Secretary of War. On the morrow, we told them, they'd at last have the chance to fire their rifles at secession and give the bayonet to treason. Without them, the Union might well be lost. The spirit of George Washington hovered above them, awaiting their decision. We spoke the same words to the Fourth Pennsylvania, and begged them to serve a single week more. In both cases, the men listened patiently, then continued making ready to leave.

The light faded. The moon came up. I rode back toward my lodgings through the encampments. Some were bedlams of noise and gaming and drunkenness. Others were quiet. One company of Scotsmen were singing "The Star-Spangled Banner" most beautifully. I moved on. In the distance a band was playing the soothing serenade from *Don Pasquale*. I couldn't help but notice the number of men clustered about the chaplains' tents. Some were shedding their sins, some dictating letters to the scribbling chaplains. I passed quite close to one and smiled to catch the words "no qualm, dearest Gwen, at dying for our precious Union."

SHEM SUGGS

It was a warm night. We knew there'd soon be a battle. The horses knew it too. Greta was restless as a flea-bit dog, stamping her hooves and flicking her tail. Most of the company played at cards. No one seemed to want to turn in. One read a letter from his father saying wars were uncivilized, low, immoral, and that civil wars were the worst of the brood. The letter was burned with great jollity. After a time, though, the men took to studying Bibles instead of poker hands. It struck me as strange that nearly all the legions of soldiers camped around me considered themselves to be whole-souled Christians, had heard preaching every Sunday of their lives, had memorized piles of Scripture verses, and yet were ready to break the commandment against killing the moment the order was given. I went walking. I came to a man who was reading *Gulliver's Travels* to a circle of listeners. I stopped and gave ear. Gulliver had come to a curious country where horses ruled and men were thought to be the foulest of beasts. The horses, wise as they were, had no wars. They could scarcely believe it when Gulliver told them that soldiers were men paid to kill each other. Then he described sabers, muskets, bullets, cannons that left the field of battle strewn with bloody limbs, and other clever inventions that had led humans to think themselves far advanced beyond horses. It was almost too frightful to laugh at. I dearly wished I might go to that land. When the man stopped reading, I promised myself that if I lived through the war I'd learn my letters and read the rest of that book. Then I visited with the horses a long spell, and tried not to think upon what was coming.

GIDEON ADAMS

The drummers began drumming. I awoke and found it was two o'clock. The whole regiment was stirring. I fried some bacon. At three we marched, if it could be called that. We groped slowly down the road through the darkness, men stumbling over each other like drunkards. It was a still summer night, the stars wondrously clear. There were no bands playing, no singing, and little talk. The waiting was over, or nearly so. For half an hour we sprawled on the ground while a cannon was eased over a rickety bridge. We pushed on. The sky began to lighten. The man beside me mumbled the twenty-third psalm without end, as if it were a charm. Finally we approached a stone bridge that crossed Bull Run. The stream murmured softly. We halted. Not a shot had been heard. General Schenck called out a command. The artillery crew put a cannon in place and loaded it with a thirty-pound ball. At six o'clock they fired.

FLORA WHEELWORTH

It was a Sunday, the twenty-first of July. I rose in the dark, studied two chapters of Exodus, then closed my eyes and started my prayers as usual. Not five minutes later a low, sullen boom sounded in the distance. I kept my eyes shut. I knew what it was without opening them. Another followed, and then a third. Then came the sharper rattling of rifles, painfully distinct. I saw my daughters' men in my mind. I left my chair, knelt on the floor, clasped my hands more tightly than before, and continued praying for a full two hours.

EDMUND UPWING

Don't speak to me of the soldiers' hard lot. I was up on my pegs before they were that morning. 'Tis a fact, solid as stone. I'd two congressmen and their wives in the coach, bound all the way to Centreville to watch the thrashing of the Rebs. All dressed in their best and fitted out with parasols and opera glasses, not forgetting two hampers of food, and champagne for toasting the victory. 'Twas dark as Hell's cellar when we left Washington. I'd thought they would sleep, but they chattered like sparrows. I caught a good deal of it, as usual. Cabmen dull witted as their nags? Don't be daft! They know more of Washington than the President. Though whenever a question is put to me, I ignore it until it's asked a fourth time, that my passengers mightn't suspect I have ears.

There were plenty of other spectators heading south. The shooting commenced as we neared Centreville. We passed through the village and found a fine grassy spot on a hill overlooking Bull Run. Every last horse and buggy for hire in Washington seemed to be there. Linen tablecloths were spread out and people of quality spread out upon 'em. My passengers were in a merry mood—all but one of the men, who let out that McDowell had been given command for no better reason than that he'd come from Ohio, whose governor had Lincoln's ear and had whispered "McDowell" in it constantly. 'Tis a fact. I feigned deafness, but took the precaution of noting our fastest route of retreat.

JUDAH JENKINS

Since before first light I'd been standing about at General Beauregard's headquarters. Of a sudden, I was ordered to ride over to Colonel Evans, near the stone bridge, and bring back word on the Yanks' position. I'd been waiting to show my worth as a courier. I galloped toward the west. It dawned upon me that I was headed straight for the fighting. It dawned on my horse as well. The musket balls began to whiz past us. He slowed, two legs moving ahead while the other two tried to retreat. I wrestled him forward, past soldiers waiting to advance. Others were firing in the woods. I spied Colonel Evans, hopped to the ground, and tied the reins tight to a tree. Just then I heard someone shout "Pull her off!" The next moment there came a tremendous roar. It was one of our cannons. A man who'd been standing too close to the muzzle was thrown twenty feet. Blood gushed out of one of his ears. I wondered if I wasn't deaf myself. Then I turned, saw the broken reins, and realized I was a courier whose horse had sprinted away.

DIETRICH HERZ

Our entire division was to march to the west, cross the stream where it was unguarded, and surprise the Rebels with an attack at dawn. This called for speed. Yet we idled an hour that morning while other troops used the narrow road. Our officers swore in German and English. General Hunter at last led us out, but took a wrong turning that doubled our march. It was nearly nine and already stifling when we finally reached Bull Run. Its waters were slow-moving and muddy. We filled our canteens, picked blueberries, then waded across, four hours late. A farmer saw us and galloped off. The Confederates must have been well warned without him. They met us with a volley of rifle fire, then artillery shells. The order was given to charge up a slope. I felt I was advancing into a dream. There were cries and explosions. The air stank of sulfur. I passed a man sitting with his intestines spread out in his lap and wondered if the sight was real.

The men about me crouched and shot. Those behind us singed our hair with their bullets. I aimed at the smoke in the distance, fired, and saw my ramrod sail through the air. I'd forgotten to take it out of the barrel. My thoughts flew suddenly to Germany, to a toy gun I'd had as a child. I saw my mother in memory, and my aunts. Then my mind went black quick as a candle blown out.

TOBY BOYCE

Of a sudden our men got the call. They were to march west and join the fight. "Aim low and trust in God," spoke an officer. "Let 'em know Georgia's here!" cried another. They formed up into ranks double quick. One soldier called Lincoln "the Illinois ape" and promised to bring back a lock of his hair. They set off smartly. All the band watched. We'd been ordered to keep far behind the fighting. Seeing them leave for battle, proud as stallions, filled me full of envy. I didn't care a cow tick for playing the fife and longed for a rifle in my hands instead. It was hard to endure. For me, leastways. Two of the horn players were drinking from flasks and toasting their wisdom at serving in the rear.

JAMES DACY

My eyes and pencil were in constant motion. Here, four cannons rumbled up the road. There, a pair of soldiers carried a wounded comrade upon their crossed rifles. Below me, a company shouted three cheers for the Union before plunging into the fray. I could scarcely contain my own excitement. After tramping across the countryside, I'd found myself a fine vantage point for observing McDowell's attack. How gallantly our men advanced into a perfect storm of bullets! The Confederates slowly began to give ground. The scene I was sketching continually changed before my eyes, like a cloud in the sky. Regiment upon regiment of Northerners rushed into the fight. I made out McDowell riding among them, in full dress and white gloves, urging them forward. I could no longer bear merely to record. I threw down my pencil, bolted to my feet, and cheered them on loudly myself.

COLONEL OLIVER BRATTLE

General Beauregard seemed to be in a state of utter confusion. Five of our brigades should have crossed Bull
Run on our right and attacked, yet we heard hardly a
shot from that quarter. Before us, at Mitchell's Ford,
where he'd expected the brunt of the Union assault,
there was little shooting as well. He stared out the windows of the house we occupied. His orders had been
maddeningly vague. Many seemed never to have been
received. We lacked for couriers and were starved for re-
ports. We who were directing the battle knew nothing!
This fog was pierced by the undeniable fact of firing far
to our left. This didn't accord with the general's plan.
He'd weighted our line heavily to the right. Grudgingly,
he sent some men west, still hoping to save his cherished offensive. The firing grew louder. I suggested he
ride out and investigate, but he ignored me. He ap-
peared paralyzed by the dilemma. General Johnston

paced in a fury. He outranked General Beauregard, but had just come by train with his troops from the west and had left the campaign's command with him. Finally, he could stand it no more. He shook his hat at the smoke in the west. "The battle is there!" he announced. "I am going!"

A. B. TILBURY

The guns did fairly roar before us. Our drivers raised a
fine roar of their own, swearing and snapping their
whips to bring our fieldpieces into position. There were
six guns in our battery, with eight men to a gun. We labored hard and fast, firing solid shot, then switched to
shrapnel. Our mothers soon wouldn't have known our
faces, black with powder and running with sweat. "May
God have mercy on their guilty souls," our lieutenant
would shout, then yank on the lanyard. I had little
leisure to watch the shells fly and could scarcely make
out the Rebels for the smoke. Then I saw that the gun
crew beside us was pointing. The enemy lines had broken and the men were scattering like rabbits. We were
ordered forward. Didn't we crow! "They're whipped!"
"Look at 'em all skedaddle!" "We'll hang Jeff Davis!" "The
war is over!"

DR. WILLIAM RYE

I lay on the grass, listening to the battle. Another doctor
stood nearby, and two or three assistants. We were before a church, some miles from the fighting. Bees buzzed
loudly from a hive nearby. A mockingbird went through
his program, his song an unending river of gladness. Our
ears, however, were cocked toward the distance. The
first great battle of the war was taking place over the
next hill. We knew the first wounded would shortly ar-
rive. We'd set up two tables and readied our tourniquets,
forceps, scalpels, and saws. We waited.

EDMUND UPWING

As the day was heartlessly hot and humid, I sat in my coach to keep out of the sun and exercised my jaws on a roll. My passengers' menu reached my nose and eyes but not, alas, my stomach. Virginia ham, softshell crabs, Chesapeake Bay oysters on ice. Some dined on pheasant. 'Tis a fact, bright as brass. They squinted at the smoke now and then, then returned to the clash of knife and fork. All at once an officer of some sort galloped up our way. "We've whipped them on all points!" he cried out. "They're retreating fast and we're after them!" He charged off again. The air rang with cheers. My passengers were so moved by the news that they filled my old tin cup with champagne.

VIRGIL PEAVEY

We'd marched five miles and were perishing for water, then reached the battle and forgot we were thirsty. The balls whistled by us. It was a new sound to me. Jack, our mascot, a brave little bulldog, snapped at the bullets as if they were flies. I grabbed my friend Tuck to show him the sight, then saw he'd been shot straight in the heart. My own heart near quit. Then the call came to charge. I'd pledged to stay by him, but hadn't calculated on him getting killed. Men scurried past. An officer shouted and shoved me ahead with the others. I dearly disliked leaving Tuck behind and suddenly felt all alone in the world. We got cut up awful and dashed back a spell later. Then we spied a gray regiment coming, almost fainted for joy, drew close by—and were killed by the cartload when they opened fire. It was Sherman's men, gray-clad same as us. We cut dirt for our lives all the way to a creek. We formed a new line, but the shells and bullets fell upon us thick as rain. Men promised out loud to quit all their vices if only the Lord would spare their lives. General Bee glared back at Jackson, who was perched with his troops on a hill out of range. "He stands there like a damned stone wall!" he cried. "Why doesn't he come and support us?" He let loose a deal of blasphemy. The next minute he was shot dead off his horse.

DIETRICH HERZ

My eyes opened and focused upon grass. I felt heavy and numb as a millstone. I was lying on the ground, tried to get up, but couldn't make my head or limbs move. I felt wet about my legs, thought it must be from blood, but couldn't tell where I'd been hit. I wondered how long I'd been lying there. The battle had moved ahead over the hill. I fixed my eyes on a man nearby. His eyes were looking straight back at me. Then I saw the red soaking through his shirt. Had the stretcher-bearers thought me dead as well? Was I wounded past helping? My head began pounding. "I mustn't die here!" I told myself. I stared at the green grass before me with envy. Then I thought of the woman who'd sewn my shirt, whose note I'd never forgotten. Her photograph was in my jacket pocket. I had no family of my own in this country, and I'd thought and worried about her as you would about a wife or relation. I spoke to her now, within my mind. I told her we were both meant to live longer. I begged her not to take her own life. I described the tuft of grass before me. I asked her to help me live.

CARLOTTA KING

I was jump-stomached all day, wonderin' who was winnin'. Past noon a soldier came wanderin' our way. He'd been shot through the ear and held a kerchief up against it, drippin' blood. I'd washed out all the master's clothes and was sittin' with the other slaves. He told us the Southern men were licked. I could hardly keep from yellin' for joy. I wouldn't have to run off to the North— the North was marchin' down to me! Some cannons fired just then, and I thought, The Lord's smitin' the South at last! The soldier shucked off his pack and sat down. He took out a mirror and studied his face. His ear had a rip. He almost cried to see it. "The Confederacy's finished," he said. "And worse than that, my good looks is gone forever!"

GIDEON ADAMS

We weren't far from the battle. It went quiet for a time, then struck up again louder than ever. I rejoiced at this. Finally, I felt sure, we'd be called to join the fight. I was wrong. We sat on the ground, an entire brigade of three thousand men, there by the stone bridge where we'd been sitting all day. Our role had been to fire a few shots and serve as decoys to mask McDowell's main attack. Had I trained for months and journeyed a thousand miles only to pretend to fight? Had we been forgotten? I boiled with disappointment. While our comrades fought for freedom and the Union, the man beside me took aim at a turkey.

JUDAH JENKINS

I never did catch up with that horse. I soon found another without a rider. There was blood on the saddle. I wiped it off and wondered if a ghost weren't watching me. We galloped back and forth, carrying orders and news, most of it bad. About noon I heard whistles at Manassas Junction. It was General Smith's regiments. They were the last of Johnston's men to make the trip from the Shenandoah. I was sent to tell them to hurry to the battle. The general saw the stragglers on the road, bleeding, crying for water, limping along or running for home like madmen. I told him the fight was all but lost. He ordered his troops to march at quickstep.

A. B. TILBURY

Twelve-pound balls, canister, shrapnel. We sent them all
at the Southerners. Then their artillery took our measure and commenced to devil us in return. We'd fire and
they'd fire. I expect they crouched when they heard a
shell coming, same as we did. I almost felt I'd a double
across the lines. I took to wondering whether their men
were truly all savages, as I'd heard tell. They pulled back
and hid their guns behind a house. Union shells ripped
right through the walls. There was a woman inside, it
turned out, and some of her kin. A man ran out, scream-
ing "They've killed my mother!" over and over. I asked
myself why soldiering was praised up as something to be
proud of. We then pulled our guns to a hill far forward,
with no infantry to protect us. We protested, but it was
McDowell's order. A line of men in blue marched toward
us. Captain Griffin swore they were Rebels, but Major
Barry swore even louder that they were our infantry

support. There was no wind at all, so their flag hung limp. We couldn't make it out, and held our fire. They came almost among us. Then the air exploded. That murderous volley dropped half our men and every last one of our horses. I was lucky to be struck only in both arms, leaving me free to run for my life.

SHEM SUGGS

We were mounted and waiting. We were tucked in the trees, ready to spring upon the Yanks. Jeb Stuart was our colonel. He did love a surprise. He was even fonder of dressing up fine, and I thought sure his duds would give us away. Gold silk sash, gold spurs, white buckskin gloves, and an ostrich plume in his hat. He squinted out between the trees. The battle was almighty thick and hot. Finally, he gave the sign. He led us out of the woods and charged down into a line of Zouaves got up even gaudier than he was. They looked as frighted as if we'd ridden up out of Hell. There were cries and shots and smoke on every side. We were packed in tight. It was one great confusion. A Yank came at me with his bayonet. I jerked the reins left and he missed my leg. Then he aimed it at my horse. I shot him without thinking. I was amazed to see him pitch back, and gawked at the blood running down his side. I could scarcely believe I was the cause. I'd shot a man, a thin man with red whiskers. I might have just made his younguns into or-phans, same as me. I felt shaky and shameful. We pulled back toward the woods. I found I was hoping the man would live.

GENERAL IRVIN McDOWELL

My flanking attack had succeeded superbly. Despite the delays, despite the fact that my men were no more than summer soldiers, despite the losses they'd absorbed, we'd driven the enemy backward all day. I paused for a time to re-form my line. I was then ready to deliver the death blow, ending the battle and the Confederacy both. Beauregard, though, had made use of the lull and had shifted many more men west. I ordered my artillery forward, to pound his line at close range. But the infantry who were to support them lost their way and were shattered by cavalry. Our gunners, through an error, were then slaughtered by the Rebels, who turned our cannons about upon us. We stormed the hill and reclaimed them more than once, but each time were forced to retreat. My men were collapsing from exhaustion and thirst. Some died of sunstroke in the fearsome heat. Fresh Southern troops, brought east by train, then reached the field, to great cheers from their comrades. I cursed old General Patterson anew. They fell upon us with their bloodcurdling yell. The right end of my line began to buckle. Then I watched it give way like a dam.

TOBY BOYCE

I didn't reckon I could bear it another minute. The very battle I'd wanted a part in was booming just a few miles off, while I sat on a log and whittled a stick. The older Georgia boys who'd joined would come home loaded down heavy as peddlers with Yankee guns and medals and glory. And with scars to put on public display. I'd stare like the rest, quiet as a clam. I'd have been there as well, but would have to ask *them* to tell me exactly what had happened. The thought chafed me fierce. I snapped my knife shut. I stood up and snuck off toward the fighting.

JAMES DACY

It takes but a pebble to start an avalanche. The sight of some of our soldiers fleeing infected all the others with fear. Just at that moment, some Union teamsters drove their empty ammunition carts feverishly away from the battle and toward the rear, in full view of our men. They lashed their horses, no doubt that they might quickly return with supplies for our gunners. The troops, though, seemed to think them in desperate flight and concluded the cause was lost. Regiments suddenly ceased to exist. A vast tide of men began streaming from the field, slowly at first, then in a mad flood. My eyes were disbelieving. My thoughts swirled. These weren't the same soldiers I'd sketched earlier. My notebook held heroes, marching in unison, bravely advancing, disdainful of death. I refused to draw the scene before me, or to sit idly by. I dashed toward the throng. I picked up a New York regimental standard flung down in the dust, and held it high. "Rally 'round, New York!" I shouted above the tumult. "Make a stand!" The men ignored me, surging past in a panic. I waved the standard back and forth. "New Yorkers, form up! Stand your ground and the day is yours! Why do you run?" "Because I can't fly!" a voice called back.

COLONEL OLIVER BRATTLE

General Beauregard's head finally cleared. He cast aside his original plan and galloped off to the battle at last. I rode with him. As new troops arrived, he fit them into our lengthening line. He heartened them in spirited fashion, especially during the worst of the fighting, riding up and down the ranks, praising the men, shoring up their resolve, instantly mounting another horse when his own was shot from beneath him. When we saw the Northerners starting to flee, he led our entire line forward in attack. President Davis arrived by train from Richmond in time to watch the rout. The speed of the Union collapse was astounding. Their soldiers left everything that might slow them. In a matter of minutes the ground they'd stood on held muskets, cannons, colors, packs, ammunition, blankets, caps—but no men.

EDMUND UPWING

The shout went 'round, "The Rebels are upon us!" The words struck the picnickers like a storm, sent them shrieking into their coaches, and sent every coach bolting toward the road. My riders commanded that I put on all speed. Each driver heard the same demand. The road was narrow and choked with coaches. This mass of wheels and whips blocked the soldiers, who seemed even more eager than we to be gone. They were furious with us. How their teamsters swore! Those on foot rushed around us like an April torrent. They were bloody, dusty, and wild-eyed as wolves. "The Black Horse Cavalry is coming!" one bellowed. The air rang with rumors of hidden batteries, heartless horsemen, rivers red with blood, and visions worthy of the Book of Revelation. One frantic soldier cut a horse free from a wagon's team and took off bareback. Another fugitive tried to unseat me. I drove him off with my whip. 'Tis a fact. Then there came a terrific boom. Women screamed. A Rebel shell had fallen on the road. The caravan halted. The way was blocked by a tangle of overturned wagons. The soldiers scattered or froze in fear. Men fled their buggies. A second shell struck. Then a young officer galloped up, leaped down, and dragged the vehicles away. His courage was acclaimed. We jerked forward afresh. My sharp ear learned that the man's name was Custer. All predicted that he was destined for great deeds.

CARLOTTA KING

A slave came and told us the Union was beat. My heart dropped like a bucket down a well. A while later the master's friends came up the road, hootin' and carryin' on over the victory, noisy as jays. I couldn't pretend smilin' and just turned away. Then one of 'em told me my master was wounded and pointed where I'd find him. I gathered up a clean suit of clothes for him and some bandages and set off. Men were ridin' or walkin' every which way. I passed into the trees. Just some dead men there. I never did find my master. Never tried to neither. I told myself I couldn't sit and wait for the Northerners to whip the South. And if Union soldiers sent slaves back to their masters, I'd just have to keep clear of 'em. I set down the clothes when I came to Bull Run. Then I waded across and kept movin' north.

DIETRICH HERZ

I came to my senses some hours later. I was shaking with cold, though the sun shone upon me. I listened and heard a few shots, very distant. The sun was much lower. It seemed days since that morning. I didn't think about the battle, about my regiment or my friends, but only of being found by someone. Then I heard a rustling. "A Barlow knife," said a voice. "Got me two more pocket watches," said another. My heart filled with hope. The ground shook around me. "Reckon I'll be ticking worse than a clock shop," the same voice went on. Then a hand reached inside my jacket. I felt the heat of the man's warm arm. I found I could now move my own arm slightly, raised a finger to show him I lived, and spoke the words "Please help me." The man gave a yelp. "Don't go!" I pleaded. But he bounded away, dropping the photograph of the seamstress on the grass. I slowly moved my arm that way, a task that seemed to take hours, and at last dropped my hand upon it and cursed the plunderer.

SHEM SUGGS

We rode off after the Northerners and took prisoners by the hundred. Some said we should march upon Washington, but our troops were dead-weary and dog-hungry. Winning had left us nearly whipped ourselves. I looked over the field. Dead horses were scattered about everywhere. Worse than them were the ones that were wounded, charging about without any rider, blood running down out their nostrils. Some who'd been hit in one leg perched on the other three, patient as you please. Some gnawed at their wounds all afrenzy. Others were under the guns they'd been hauling, crushed to death or squealing like pigs. I saw one, alive and looking about, hitched to a team of five others, all dead. I hadn't much stomach for celebrating. I ate some hardtack and emptied my canteen. Then I found a spade and began burying horses.

NATHANIEL EPP

The bands had been left in Centreville that morning. They gave us a grand serenade all day, practicing up for their march into Richmond. Then the troops began streaming back our way. I was baffled. I'd expected to trail them south, taking piles of pictures of soldiers standing on captured flags and such. It was plain that these men had no desire to stop and sit for their portraits. They swept through as if the Devil were reaching for 'em. Those in the bands picked up the panic, threw down their instruments without a care, and jumped onto the backs of the teamsters' horses. I thought upon the matter a moment, then took a stroll, sat under a tree, and dined on some turkey and wine left behind by the society folks. I'd no cause to flee. The Rebels who were coming would be anxious to have their pictures made.

DR. WILLIAM RYE

There were moments when my mind turned away from my work and imagined the rejoicing in Richmond. I saw the men packing the bar of the Spotswood Hotel, heard the crowds singing in the streets. Then my eyes returned to the crowd around me, sprawled on the ground, bloody, groaning, fanning the clouds of flies from their wounds or unconscious and unaware of their presence. We soon ran out of chloroform and whiskey and had to hold the men down while operating. We probed and sawed and stitched without stop and were soon as blood-covered as they were. A small mountain of amputated limbs grew up between our two tables, the feet often still bearing shoes. A few of the hands wore gloves. The sights and the stench were overpowering. A detachment of cavalry passing the scene bent over their pommels and retched, to a man. A victory? Indeed it was, for Death upon his pale horse.

GIDEON ADAMS

We plodded past abandoned artillery, ammunition boxes, knapsacks beyond number, past mounds of flour and sugar and pork spilling out of broken barrels, cast out of wagons to make room for men. One private in my company loudly claimed that every army that had launched an attack on the Sabbath had been defeated. "The finger of the Almighty is in it!" he declared. The man beside me seemed in high spirits and clapped me on the shoulder. "Well, Able, we'll be back in Ohio in a week," he said. His good cheer repelled me. I'd never become accustomed to my new name. But I determined that moment that I'd continue to use it, that I'd join a three-year regiment, and that I wouldn't return to Ohio until the Rebels had been beaten. This vow quickened my step, putting the dismal defeat farther behind me. I itched for the next battle to begin.

TOBY BOYCE

By the time I got there, the fighting was done with. That griped me. Then I spied a knife, the long sort the soldiers called Arkansas toothpicks. I snatched it up. I had me a souvenir to show off at home and felt better. I kept on, wondering what else I might find. I came on a dead man, half a biscuit in his hand and the other half clamped in his teeth. I turned away. A voice asked for water. I hadn't any and scurried on. I finally came to Bull Run. Loads of Union men, shot or drowned trying to cross, lay all about. Then a voice said "Boy." I turned and saw a man who'd no body to speak of below his waist. "Shoot me," he said. He pointed to his rifle. My stomach emptied. He was a Yank. How I'd longed back home to kill one. Here I finally had my chance. But instead I ran, dodging dead bodies, ran back through the Southern men, past the wagons, past the doctors, and kept on running toward Georgia and Grandpap.

EDMUND UPWING

Rain came on during the night. It soaked the men, turned the roads to muck, and added more misery to the retreat. It was past midnight when we reached Washington. All that night and the following day the soldiers trudged across the Long Bridge, sodden, sullen, the very picture of defeat. They dropped asleep on sidewalks and porches. Kindhearted women made vats of soup, set them by the street, and fed the famished lads. Staggering along through the rain, they looked a parade of ghosts. 'Tis a fact. My eyes shall never forget it. Nor my ears. How my passengers railed against the soldiers! And their know-nothing officers, and the profiteers, and the press, and the generals, and the President. I learned later that week that Jeff Davis and Beauregard were pulled to pieces the same way for not pressing on toward Washington. A few days after the battle, Lincoln sent McDowell packing. This raised spirits some, but not everyone's. I heard that Horace Greeley himself, the most powerful editor in the land—who'd first told Lincoln to let the South secede, then insisted that Richmond be taken—now had sent Lincoln a letter stating that the Rebels couldn't be beaten! The winds blew fickle about the President, but he had his feet on the ground. I'm proud to say he ignored the letter.

FLORA WHEELWORTH

The first wagonload of wounded arrived that afternoon. By night, every bed and settee and most of the floor was occupied by wounded soldiers. The other houses nearby were the same. The three servants and I did all we could, cleaning the men and their ghastly wounds, changing dressings, feeding, giving comfort. I was told that my eldest daughter's husband had been wounded, and I gave the men the same care that I prayed he was receiving. Several were Yankees. We attended them with no less solicitude. They were all simply men, all in grave need. When they died, as so many did, they seemed changed from men back into infants, their bodies relaxing just like a babe's settling into its slumber. We saved locks of hair to send to their families, and the shirts the men had worn as well, which we labored to cleanse of blood. If I slept an hour or more straight through at night, I considered myself blessed. The rooms stirred endlessly with voices. One man asked for "Clarissa" without cease. Others moaned constantly for water. An officer called out, "Open the door to the King of Glory" and died the next instant. One Union man, a German I believe, both legs shattered and shot through the neck, clutched a photograph of a woman and would not be parted from it, even in sleep. Perhaps it did have healing powers. He had both legs taken off by a doctor who came to us, and survived the ordeal.

LILY MALLOY

We hadn't known there'd been a battle until a week after it was over. Everyone was greatly cast down by the news of the Union's defeat. Some feared that the war might not end until Christmas. The following week Father brought home a letter informing us that Patrick had been killed in the course of the battle. It was from his captain. It said he'd fought bravely, had been given a fine burial, and was mourned and missed by all who'd known him. Mother wailed. Father looked almost smug, as if Patrick had been punished, as promised. I felt turned to granite by the news, then dashed outside toward the wheat field. I ran without thinking, for miles it seemed, then fell down, hidden by the long wheat, and cried until my ribs ached. I tried to picture his dying, his body, his face, his grave, but couldn't. He'd been killed on a Sunday. I tried to recall it. We'd gone to church, then come home and studied our Bibles in silence, as always. It seemed impossible that on a day so quiet there'd been a battle anywhere. I felt a great hatred for the stream called Bull Run. I thought back to walking through the wheat when it had been shorter, weeks before. How I yearned to be that girl again, back before Patrick had been killed! I begged for us both to be returned to that time, over and over again, until the sky began to darken. Then I climbed to my knees, then my feet, stood for a while, wobble-legged, and slowly headed back. I'd talked to Patrick in the fields that summer. I'd fancied he heard me, far as he was. He was now ever more distant still. I wondered whether he could hear me now. I spoke to him all the long walk home.

NOTE

The speakers in this book, except for General McDowell, are fictional. The background, however, is factual, from whiskey hidden in watermelons to the details of the battle.

For those who wish to stage this work or perform it as readers' theater, the following synopsis will make it easier to locate the various parts.

More award-winning titles from

Paul Fleischman

Published by
Harper Trophy Paperback Books

Historical fiction as only Paul Fleischman could write it

The Borning Room

It's a place where life and love begin, and loss is borne. Mothers give birth in the borning room. The dying take their departure there.

Outside the Lott family's Ohio farmhouse, the Civil War rages, slavery falls, and the world marvels at the wonder of electricity. Inside, within the walls of the borning room, Georgina Lott will experience her life's greatest turnings. Across the years, she discovers womanhood and first love, experiences the mourning that comes with loss, and, as did her mother and grandmother, at last takes her place in the room as another precious life is about to begin.

"A fine novel that combines the immediacy of personal experience with a sense of the changes and the continuity that make up our lives. First-rate."

—*The New Yorker*

""Exquisite. . . . An intimate and memorable portrayal of a stalwart family . . . a book not to be missed."

(Starred review)—*The Horn Book*

A 1991 Golden Kite Award Honor Book for Fiction (SCBW)
A Notable Children's Book (ALA)
A Best Book for Young Adults (ALA)

A Charlotte Zolotow Book

Saturnalia

December, 1681. As darkness falls and the bone-cracking chill of winter settles over Boston, a boy as tall and thin as a spring shoot slips stealthily out of his master's house. By day, he is William, the printer's knowledgeable apprentice. By night, he is Weetasket of the Narraganset tribe, who bravely risks the magistrate's wrath to search for his brother—and his own Indian past.

In the Puritan town, where masters and servants inhabit two very different worlds, only William walks in both . . . until the fateful night of the Saturnalia, the ancient Roman holiday on which masters and slaves trade roles. It is a night that will end in triumph and tragedy, as the slaving, dreaming, courting, and conniving of each caste is revealed to the other . . . and as the strong light of truth is shed on the colonials' faith, their follies, and the dark deeds of their Indian wars.

"Provocative and rewarding."   —*The New York Times*

"An amusing satiric novel full of atmosphere and suspense."   —*The New Yorker*

A Notable Children's Book (ALA)

1990 *Boston Globe–Horn Book* Award for Fiction

A Charlotte Zolotow Book

Poetry as readers' theater: Paul Fleischman's poems for two voices

Joyful Noise
Poems for Two Voices

Written to be read aloud by two voices—sometimes alternating, sometimes simultaneous—here are irresistible poems that celebrate the insect world, from the short life of the mayfly to the love song of the book louse. Funny, sad, loud, and quiet, these poems resound with a booming, boisterous, joyful noise.

"This marvelous, lyrical evocation of the insect world demands accolades. Each selection is a gem, polished to perfection."   —*The Horn Book*

Winner of the 1989 Newbery Medal

A Notable Children's Book (ALA)

A Best Book for Young Adults (ALA)

1988 *Boston Globe-Horn Book* Award
Honor Book for Fiction/Poetry

A Charlotte Zolotow Book

I Am Phoenix
Poems for Two Voices

In this companion volume to JOYFUL NOISE: *Poems for Two Voices*, the winner of the 1989 Newbery Medal, Paul Fleischman celebrates the sound, the sense, the essence of birds. Written to be spoken aloud by two voices, sometimes alternating, sometimes simultaneous, these poems perfectly capture the beauty of birds in their singing, soaring, and rejoicing.

A Charlotte Zolotow Book